THE MAN IN THE IRON MASK

Vol. 3: The Iron Mask

Adapted from the novel by ALEXANDRE DUMAS

THE STORY SO FAR:

In the 17th century, Athos, Porthos, and Aramis—famed as "The Three Musketeers"—were joined in friendship by young d'Artagnan, in service to King Louis XIII of France. Three decades later, Athos had become a count—Porthos, by marriage, a baron—and shrewd Aramis, the Bishop of Vannes. D'Artagnan now commanded the Musketeers.

Aramis learned that one Philippe, a prisoner in the Bastille, was actually the twin brother of King Louis XIV, held in seclusion since his birth 25 years before, lest knowledge of his existence lead to civil war. Aramis spirited Philippe from prison and kept him in hiding. He convinced Nicholas Fouquet, the nation's Surintendant (collector of taxes), to throw a huge fête at his vast estate, Vaux-le-Vicomte, in the King's honor…at a time when Fouquet's rival, finance minister Jean-Baptiste Colbert, had convinced Louis that Fouquet was treasonously corrupt.

That night, after the festivities, the King was kidnapped by Aramis and his uncomprehending dupe, Porthos, and exchanged for his twin. Philippe slept that night in the royal bedchamber at Vaux—while a miserable Louis spent the night in a cell at the Bastille….

Writer	Special Thanks	Penciler	Inker
Roy Thomas	Deborah Sherer & Freeman Henry	Hugo Petrus	Tom Palmer

Colorist	Letterer	Cover	Special Thanks
June Chung	Virtual Calligraphy's Joe Caramagna	Marko Djurdjevic	Chris Allo

Production	Associate Editor	Editor	Editor in Chief	Publisher
Anthony Dial	Nicole Boose	Ralph Macchio	Joe Quesada	Dan Buckley

Library of Congress Cataloging-in-Publication Data

Thomas, Roy, 1940-
  The man in the iron mask / adapted from the novel by Alexandre Dumas ; Roy Thomas, writer ; Hugo Petrus, penciler ; Tom Palmer, inker ; Virtual Calligraphy's Joe Caramagna, letterer ; June Chung, colorist. -- Reinforced library bound ed.
      v. cm.
  "Marvel."
  Contents: v. 1. The three musketeers -- v. 2. High treason -- v. 3. The iron mask -- v. 4. The man in the iron mask -- v. 5. The death of a titan -- v. 6. Musketeers no more.
  ISBN 9781599615943 (v. 1) -- ISBN 9781599615950 (v. 2) -- ISBN 9781599615967 (v. 3) -- ISBN 9781599615974 (v. 4) -- ISBN 9781599615981 (v. 5) -- ISBN 9781599615998 (v. 6)
  Summary: Retells, in comic book format, Alexandre Dumas' tale of political intrigue, romance, and adventure in seventeenth-century France.
  [1. Dumas, Alexandre, 1802-1870.--Adaptations. 2. Graphic novels. 3. Adventure and adventurers--Fiction. 4. France--History--Louis XIII, 1610-1643--Fiction.] I. Dumas, Alexandre, 1802-1870. II. Petrus, Hugo. VI. Title.
PZ7.7.T518 Man 2009
[Fic]--dc22   2008035321

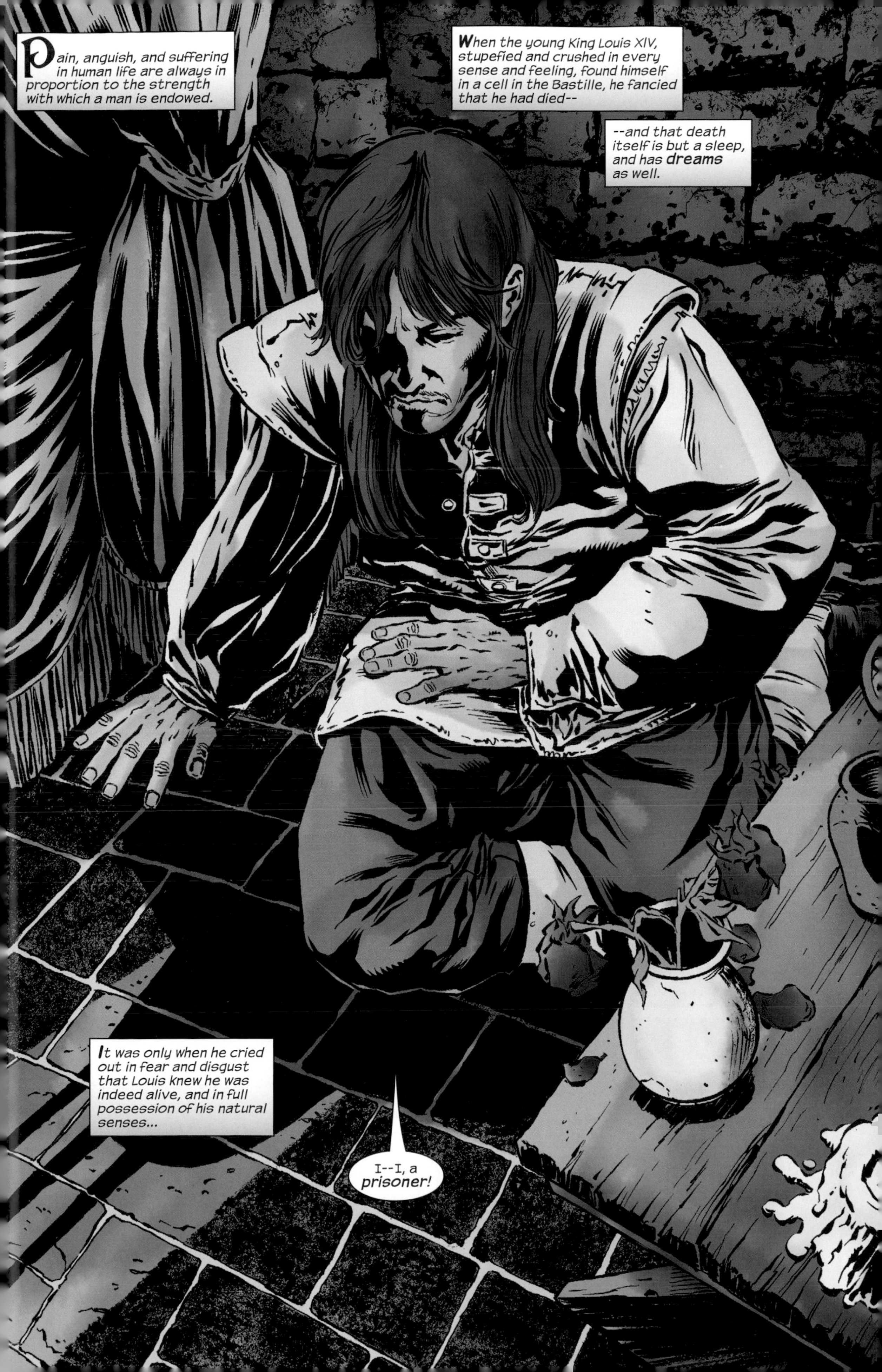
Pain, anguish, and suffering in human life are always in proportion to the strength with which a man is endowed.
When the young King Louis XIV, stupefied and crushed in every sense and feeling, found himself in a cell in the Bastille, he fancied that he had died--
--and that death itself is but a sleep, and has dreams as well.
It was only when he cried out in fear and disgust that Louis knew he was indeed alive, and in full possession of his natural senses...
I--I, a prisoner!

Colbert was right-- Monsieur Fouquet must have drawn me to Vaux, as into a snare.

But he cannot have been acting alone.

I recognized the voice of M. d'Herblay* beneath that mask.

*Aramis.

There is a governor in this place.

I will summon him to me!

The shattering of the chair awakened many a mournful echo in the profound depths of the staircase...

SMASH

...but from a human creature, not one.

This was a fresh proof for the King of the slight regard in which he was held at the Bastille.

Remarking a barred window...

...Louis began to call out, at first gently enough...

...then louder, and louder still.

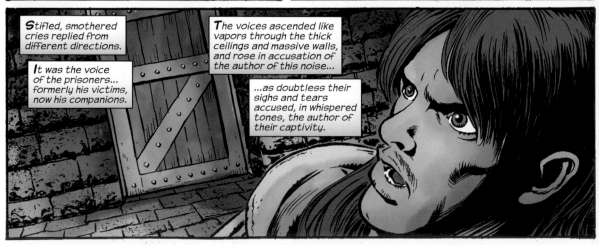

Stifled, smothered cries replied from different directions.

It was the voice of the prisoners... formerly his victims, now his companions.

The voices ascended like vapors through the thick ceilings and massive walls, and rose in accusation of the author of this noise...

...as doubtless their sighs and tears accused, in whispered tones, the author of their captivity.

After having deprived so many people of their liberty...

...the King now came among them to rob them of their rest.

This idea almost drove him mad.

What is the matter with you this morning?

Monsieur-- are you the governor of the Bastille?

You have always been very quiet and reasonable, Marchiali--but you are getting vicious, it seems.

There is no reason why you should make such a terrible disturbance.

Desire the governor to come to me!

If I even thought of disturbing him...

...he would merely send you off to one of the lower dungeons.

Two hours afterward, Louis could not have been recognized as a king...

...a gentleman...

...a human being.

He might, rather, be called a madman.

And so the bright orb of approaching day shone down upon the hated Bastille...

...and upon the singular magnificence of the Château de Vaux-le-Vicomte.

Philippe had slept uneasily, sheltered beneath his stolen crown.

Then, towards the morning...

...a shadow, rather than a body, glided into the royal chamber...

Well, M. d'Herblay?

Well, sire, all is done. The governor of the Bastille suspected nothing.

The resemblance between us, however--

That was the cause of the success.

In a few days, we will send the captive to a place of exile so distant that the duration of human life would not be enough to allow his return.

And what is to be done with the Baron du Vallon?*

Why... confer a dukedom upon him, I suppose.

*Porthos.

A step... in the vestibule...

Louis bade my captain of the Musketeers arrest M. Fouquet, and report here at the break of day.

D'Artagnan is a most punctual man.

But if he enters this room this morning, he will be sure to detect something that happened here.

But how can I send him away, since "I" have given him the rendezvous?

I will take care of that.

NOK NOK

Good morning, dear d'Artagnan.

Aramis! You here?

His Majesty desires you to report that he is still sleeping, after having been greatly fatigued during the whole night.

I have here an order of His Majesty, which concerns M. Fouquet.

I will go with you, for I wish to be a witness of his delight.

Minutes later, in the chamber of the Surintendant...

I am *free!?*

Yes, M. Fouquet... by the King's order.

You may thank the Bishop of Vannes, for it is to him that you owe the change that has taken place in His Majesty.

But how, Aramis, have you managed to become the King's favorite--you who have never spoken to him more than twice in your life?

Ah, the fact is that I have seen him more than a hundred times...only we have kept it very secret.

Then, perceiving that Aramis and Fouquet desired to speak in private, d'Artagnan took his leave...

Now, my dear d'Herblay, I think you should explain...

...why the King has set me at liberty, when only last night he ordered my arrest?

Colbert had convinced him I was a thief...nor did the King like *you*, I know.

The King will like me *now*.

Nor will he be, any longer, your powerful and implacable enemy.

But what happened to change things?

Do you remember the birth of Louis XIV?

This is where my secret begins.

The Queen, you must know, instead of being delivered of one son, was delivered of *two*.

What?

And the second is dead?

No. Both the children grew up--the one on the throne--

--the other, brought up in the country, then thrown into the Bastille at the age of fifteen.

The King's mother, Anne of Austria, knew it all... the King, absolutely nothing.

Ah, now I understand!

You threatened to reveal that secret, and that is why you now have the King in your power!

You understand nothing as yet.

God had formed these twins so miraculously like each other that it would be utterly impossible to distinguish the one from the other.

"Yet one has sat upon the throne of France these past several years...

"...while the other, who is, most incontestably, superior in every way to his brother, has been a prisoner of the Bastille.

There is a further inequality between them, which concerns yourself.

Between those twin sons of Louis XIII, the one who has been in prison does not know M. Colbert.

I understand you now, at last.

You are proposing a conspiracy to me?

You propose that I should agree to the substitution of one son of Louis XIII for another upon the throne?

It is already done.

The King of yesterday has gone to take his place in the Bastille which his victim has occupied for such a long time past.

And you committed such an action-- here, at my own home?

Here at Vaux, in the Chamber of Morpheus.

Last night, between twelve and one o'clock.

You have *dishonored* me in committing so foul an act of treason--so heinous a crime!

He was my guest--my sovereign--peacefully reposing beneath my roof!

Have I a man out of his senses to deal with here?

You have an *honorable man* to deal with.

You are mad!

A man who will prevent you from consummating your crime.

A man who would far sooner die--who would *kill you*, even--rather than allow you to complete his dishonor!

Reflect, monseigneur, upon everything we have to expect.

As the matter now stands, the King is still alive, and his imprisonment saves your life.

You may have been acting on my behalf--but I do not accept your services.

Yet, I do not wish your ruin...

You will leave this house.

You must leave *France!*

Upon the word of Fouquet, no one--not even the King's men--shall follow you before the expiration of four hours' time.

Four hours?

It is more time than you will need to get on board a vessel and flee to *Belle-Isle*...which I give you as a place of refuge.

Go, d'Herblay--go! As long as I live, not a hair of your head shall be injured.

Aramis replied with a cold irony of manner.

Thank you.

Now we both must hasten away--you to save your life, I to save my honor.

As Fouquet hurried off to order his best horses, Aramis knew he could not warn Philippe and take him along to Belle-Isle...

Else war would follow-- civil war, implacable in its nature.

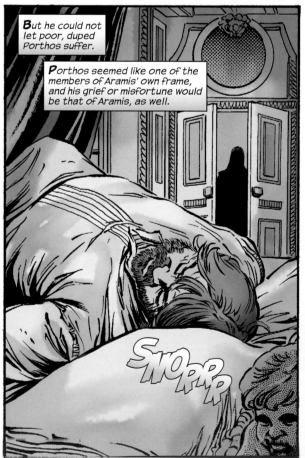

But he could not let poor, duped Porthos suffer.

Porthos seemed like one of the members of Aramis' own frame, and his grief or misfortune would be that of Aramis, as well.

SNORRR

Come, Porthos... come.

We are going off... mounted, and faster than we have ever gone in our lives.

Ahh...?

Porthos obeyed, rising from his bed even before his intelligence seemed to be aroused...and Aramis helped the giant to dress himself...

What the devil are you doing there in such an agitated manner?

We are going off on a mission of great importance, d'Artagnan.

I would far sooner be fast asleep...but the service of the King...

I have seen M. Fouquet, this very minute, ride off in a carriage.

What did he say to you?

Adieu...nothing more. Am I worth his speaking to, now that you have got into such high favor?

I predict that something will happen today which will increase your importance more than ever.

D'Artagnan gazed after his two old friends until they were out of sight.

They were going on a mission, they said...

But they looked more as if they were making an escape.

All the while, Fouquet tore along toward Paris as fast as his horses could drag him...even as he trembled with horror at what had just been revealed to him...

What must have been, he thought, the youth of those extraordinary men, who, even as age is stealing fast upon them, still are able to conceive such plans...

...and carry them out without flinching?

The Surintendant arrived at the Bastille, having traveled at the rate of five leagues and a half per hour.

Baisemeaux, governor of the prison, recognized him immediately.

But he had his orders...

Monseigneur, you know that no one can see any of the prisoners without an express order from the King.

You will let me see the prisoner called Marchiali-- *now*--

--or I will return at the head of ten thousand men and thirty pieces of cannon!

C-come with me to the keep, monseigneur, and you shall see him at once.

This job will *kill* me, I am sure it will!

Minutes later, the door to a certain cell flew open...

The King-- in this state!?

Monsieur Fouquet...

Have you come to assassinate me?

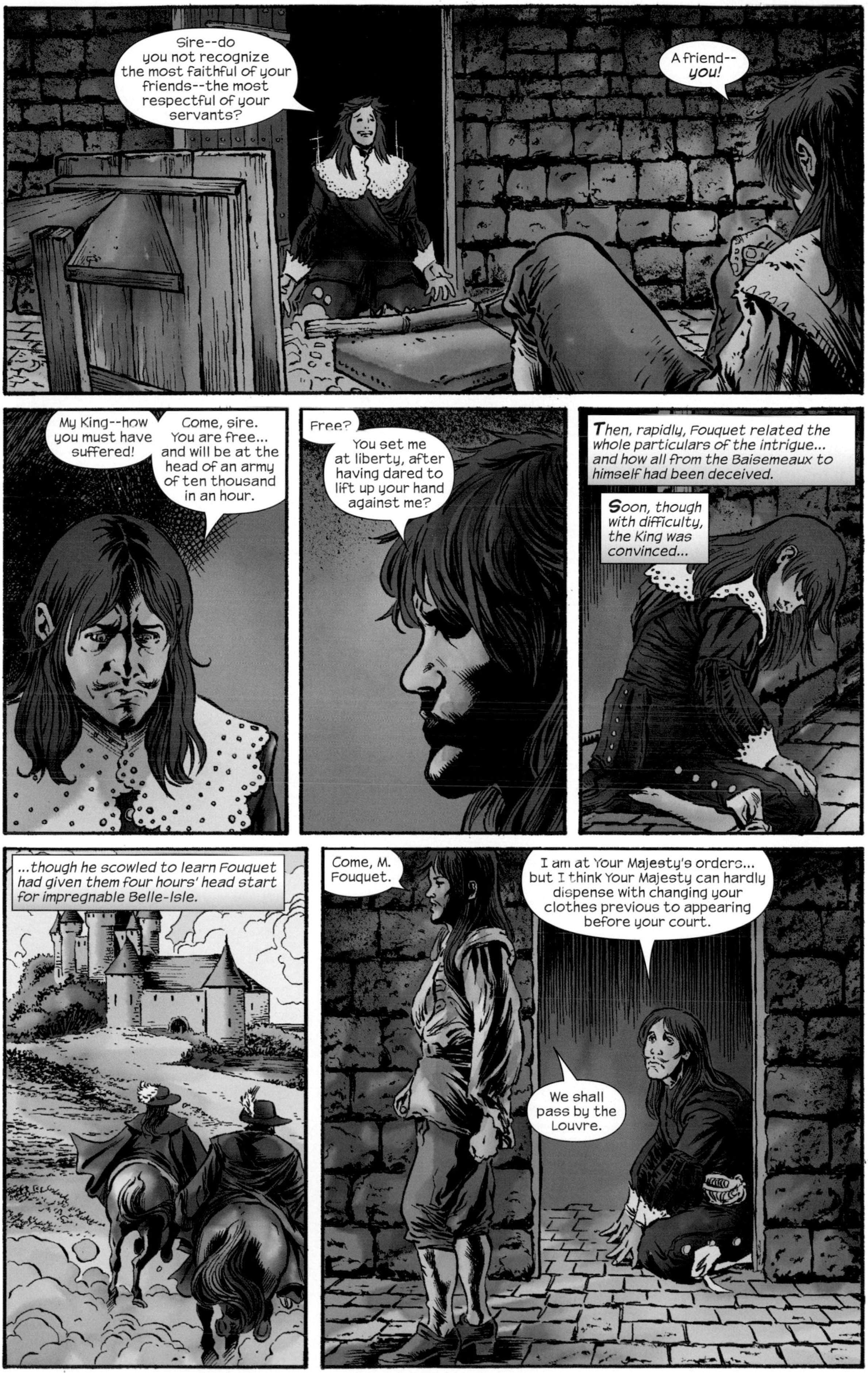

Sire--do you not recognize the most faithful of your friends--the most respectful of your servants?
A friend-- you!
My King--how you must have suffered!
Come, sire. You are free... and will be at the head of an army of ten thousand in an hour.
Free?
You set me at liberty, after having dared to lift up your hand against me?
Then, rapidly, Fouquet related the whole particulars of the intrigue... and how all from the Baisemeaux to himself had been deceived.
Soon, though with difficulty, the King was convinced...
...though he scowled to learn Fouquet had given them four hours' head start for impregnable Belle-Isle.
Come, M. Fouquet.
I am at Your Majesty's orders... but I think Your Majesty can hardly dispense with changing your clothes previous to appearing before your court.
We shall pass by the Louvre.

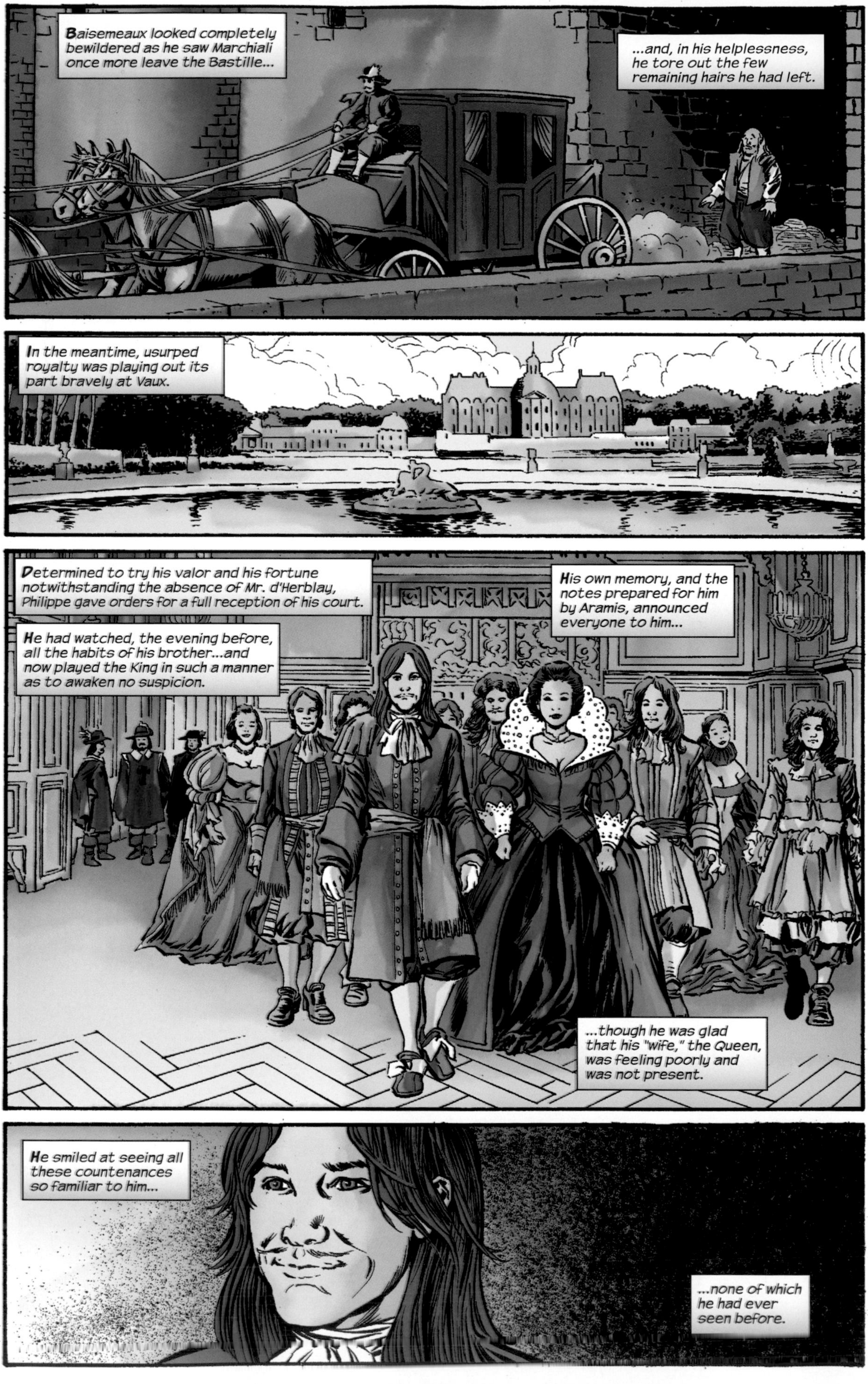
Baisemeaux looked completely bewildered as he saw Marchiali once more leave the Bastille...
...and, in his helplessness, he tore out the few remaining hairs he had left.
In the meantime, usurped royalty was playing out its part bravely at Vaux.
Determined to try his valor and his fortune notwithstanding the absence of Mr. d'Herblay, Philippe gave orders for a full reception of his court.
He had watched, the evening before, all the habits of his brother...and now played the King in such a manner as to awaken no suspicion.
His own memory, and the notes prepared for him by Aramis, announced everyone to him...
...though he was glad that his "wife," the Queen, was feeling poorly and was not present.
He smiled at seeing all these countenances so familiar to him...
...none of which he had ever seen before.

He contemplated his brother, M. de Saint-Aignan, who had usurped nothing from him.

Philippe promised himself to be a kind brother to this Prince who required nothing but gold to minister to his pleasures...

...and he tremblingly held out his hand to Henrietta, his sister-in-law, whose beauty struck him.

Yet he saw in the eyes of that Princess an expression of coldness.

Then, his mother, Anne of Austria, began a dissertation on the welcome M. Fouquet had given to the House of France, mixing hostilities with compliments...

Well, my son...are you convinced with regard to M. Fouquet and his thieving?

Madame, I do not like to hear M. Fouquet ill-spoken of.

It is a fact-- he is ruining the State.

I will hear no more concerning pretended robberies the Surintendant is falsely said to have committed.

Mother, I wish only for you to make your peace with M. Fouquet.

The Queen-Mother did not realize that, in that kiss, there was a pardon for six years of horrible suffering.

What is Your Majesty looking for? Your eyes turn constantly toward the door.

My sister, I am expecting a most distinguished man...

...a most able counselor, whom I wish to present to all, recommending him to your good graces.

Ah! Come in then, d'Artagnan.

What does Your Majesty wish?

I am waiting for your friend, the Bishop of Vannes. Let him be sought for.

D'Artagnan, reflecting that Aramis had left upon a mission, concluded that the King wished to preserve the secret of it.

Sire...does Your Majesty absolutely require M. d'Herblay to be brought to you?

No...but if he can be found...

This way! This way! A few steps more, sire!

Ah! The voice of M. Fouquet.

Then M. d'Herblay cannot be far off.

But M. Fouquet was only the second man to enter...as Louis XIV showed himself pale and frowning in the doorway...

And, in the light admitted through half-closed shutters, he appeared as luminous as if he had been enlightened by the sun.

This madness must cease!

The Queen-Mother, who perceived one Louis XIV even as she held the arm of another, uttered a little cry... as if she had beheld a phantom.

Others of the court, bewildered, kept turning their heads in astonishment from one to the other...

...or thought they saw the form of the King somehow reflected in a glass...

...as the two Louises measured each other with their looks, and darted their eyes into each other like poniards.

Yet, even then, Anne of Austria did not guess the truth...

...and others could not know it.

My mother, do you not acknowledge your *son*--

--since everyone here has forgotten his *King*?

But Philippe, even in drawing back, responded with a calm voice...

My mother--

--do you not acknowledge your *son*?

Please... I...

Ooohhhh...

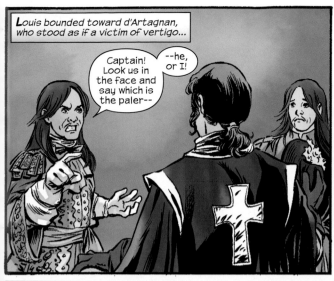

Louis bounded toward d'Artagnan, who stood as if a victim of vertigo...

Captain! Look us in the face and say which is the paler--

--he, or I!

Then, without hesitation, d'Artagnan walked straight up to Philippe...

Monsieur...

You are my prisoner!

Casting down his eyes against Philippe's reproachful stare, Louis led M. de Sainte-Aignan and his wife from the room...

...as Philippe approached Anne of Austria.

If I were not your son, I should curse you, my mother, for having rendered me...

...so unhappy.

Excuse me, monseigneur. I am but a soldier, and my oaths are his who has just left the chamber.

Thank you, M. d'Artagnan. But what is become of M. d'Herblay?

M. d'Herblay is in safety, monseigneur...

...and no one, while I live and am free, shall cause a hair to fall from his head.

M. Fouquet...

Pardon me, monseigneur, but he who has just gone out was my guest.

Here are brave friends and good hearts.

They make me regret the world.

On, M. d'Artagnan. I follow you.

At that moment, M. Colbert appeared in the doorway...

M. d'Artagnan...

...I have come to remit to you an order from the King.

What is it?

Read, monseigneur.

M. d'Artagnan will conduct the prisoner to the Ile Sainte-Marguerite.

He will cover his face with an iron visor, which the prisoner cannot raise without peril to his life.

Louis

That is just.

I am ready.

NEXT:
THE MAN IN THE
IRON MASK